Daddy Makes the Best Spaghetti

Daddy Makes the Best Spaghetti

Anna Grossnickle Hines

Clarion Books/New York

for my mother
with love

Clarion Books
a Houghton Mifflin Company imprint
215 Park Avenue South, New York, NY 10003
Copyright © 1986 by Anna Grossnickle Hines.
All rights reserved.
For information about permission to reproduce
selections from this book, write to Permissions,
Houghton Mifflin Company, 2 Park Street, Boston, MA 02108
Printed in the USA

Library of Congress Cataloging in Publication Data
Hines, Anna Grossnickle.
Daddy makes the best spaghetti.
Summary: Not only does Corey's father make the
best spaghetti, but he also dresses up like Bathman
and acts like a barking dog.
[1. Fathers—Fiction] I. Title.
PZ7.H572Dad 1986   [E]   85-13993
ISBN 0-89919-388-9   PA ISBN 0-89919-794-9

WOZ 10 9 8 7 6

When Daddy picks me up at the day-care center and takes me to the grocery store he says, "Well, Corey, what shall we have for dinner?"

"Spaghetti," I say. Daddy makes the best spaghetti.

He lets me push the cart and I remind him not to forget
the hamburger.
Sometimes Daddy plays a joke on me…

"How much for this sack of potatoes?" he asks.
"Those are free today," says the clerk.
"Great bargain," Daddy says. "I'll take them."
He's so silly!

At home I help Daddy cook. I find the right lids for the pots. I wash the vegetables.

And I set the table, one, two, three. One for Daddy.
One for Mommy. One for me.

When Mommy comes home she says, "Hello, Dears."
Daddy makes antlers and gives her a kiss.

"Ummm!" Mommy says. "Something smells good."
"It's spaghetti," I say, "and I helped."

Mommy gives us hugs and we give her some dinner.
"This spaghetti is especially good," she says.

After dinner I help Mommy with the dishes. I like to make lots of bubbles.
"Look, Mommy!"

"Looks like a bubble mountain," she says.
"Look at our bubble mountain, Daddy," I say.
But Daddy's gone.

"Oh oh," I say. "I think it's happening again." Mommy makes big eyes.

Then in comes....Ta da! Ta daaaa!...Bathman!

He swoops me up and flies me right to the tub.

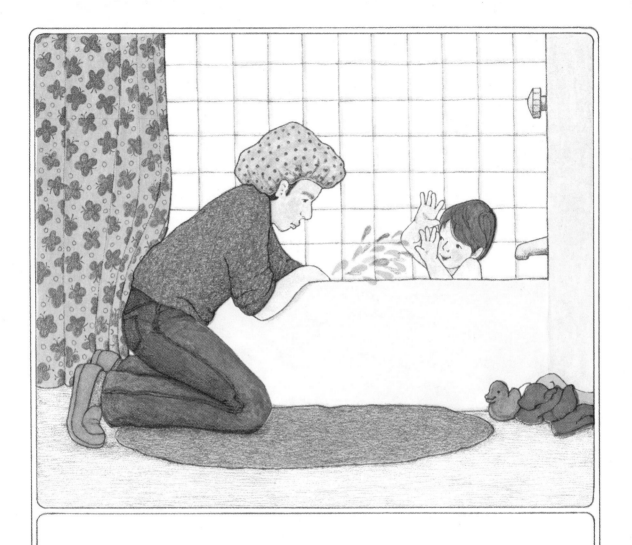

He makes the boats go so fast they splash.

Then the washcloth turns into a sea monster that
nibbles my toes and ears and nose.
"Stop monster!" I say. "It tickles!"

I get lost in the great big towel. "Oh no!" Daddy says. "I've lost Corey. What will Mommy say? And who will help me make spaghetti?"

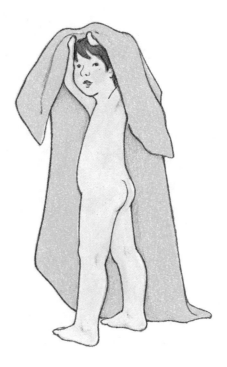

So I pop out and say, "Don't worry. I will."
But Daddy's gone.

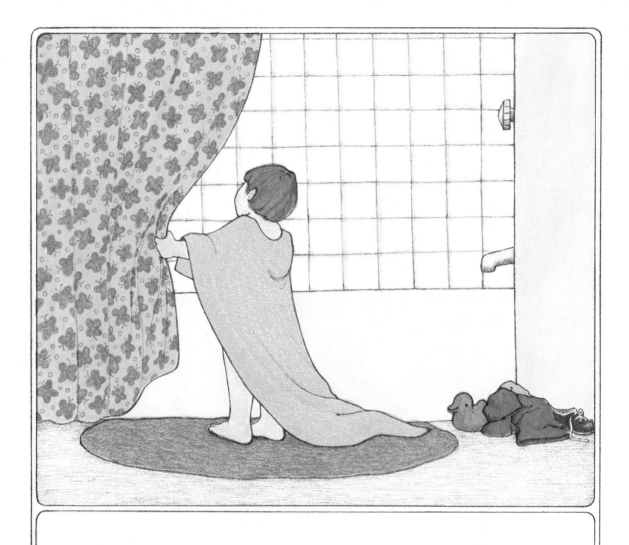

Where can he be? Not behind the shower curtain. Not behind the door.

Not in the hallway. "Oh oh…"

"Woof! Woof!"

"Oh silly dog! Those aren't ears," I say.
"They're feet!"
"I don't believe it!" Daddy says.

So I show him how they go.
Snap! Snap! Snap! And I'm all done.

"I'm done, too," says Mommy and we sit on the
couch…one, two, three…with me all cozy in between
while Mommy reads a story.

Then Daddy carries me in to bed,

Mommy tucks me in,

and we have kisses…one, two, three.
One for Mommy…one for Daddy…

Two for me!